D1094924

# MESSER

# MARCO POLO

# Messer Marco Polo

### BY
### DONN BYRNE

MODERN LIBRARY · NEW YORK

*Random House* IS THE PUBLISHER OF

# THE MODERN LIBRARY

**BENNETT A. CERF · DONALD S. KLOPFER · ROBERT K. HAAS**

Manufactured in the United States of America

Printed by Parkway Printing Company     Bound by H. Wolff

# BRIAN OSWALD DONN-BYRNE

(1889-1928)

## A NOTE ON THE AUTHOR OF
*MESSER MARCO POLO*

So Celtic in feeling and atmosphere are the stories of Donn Byrne that many of his devotees have come to believe that he never lived anywhere but in Ireland. Actually, Donn Byrne was born in New York City. Shortly after his birth, however, his parents took him back to the land of his forefathers. There he was educated and came to know the people of whom he wrote so magically. At Dublin University his love for the Irish language and for a good fight won him many prizes, first as a writer in Gaelic and second as the University's lightweight boxing champion. After continuing his studies at the Sorbonne and the University of Leipzig, he returned to the United States, where, in 1911, he married and established a home in Brooklyn Heights. He earned his living, while trying to write short stories, as an editor of dictionaries. Soon his tales began to attract attention and he added to his collection of boxing prizes many others won in short-story contests. When *Messer Marco Polo* appeared in 1921 his reputation in the literary world was firmly established. Thereafter whatever he wrote was hailed enthusiastically by his ever-growing public, until 1928, when his tragic death in an automobile accident cut short the career of one of America's best-loved story-tellers.

# MESSER MARCO POLO

THE message came to me, at the second check of the hunt, that a countryman and a clansman needed me. The ground was heavy, the day raw, and it was a drag, too fast for fun and too tame for sport. So I blessed the countryman and the clansman, and turned my back on the field.

But when they told me his name, I all but fell from the saddle.

"But that man's dead!"

But he was n't dead. He was in New York. He was traveling from the craigs of Ulster to his grandson, who had an orange-grove on the Indian River, in Florida. He was n't dead. And I said to myself with impatience, "Must every man born ninety years ago be dead?"

"But this is a damned thing," I thought, "to be saddled with a man over ninety years old. To have to act as *garde-mal-ade* at my age! Why could n't he have stayed and died at home? Sure, one of these days he will die, as we all die, and the ghost of him will never be content on the sluggish river, by the mossy trees, where the blue herons and the white cranes and the great gray pelicans fly. It will be going back, I know, to the boom-ing surf and the red-berried rowan-trees and the barking eagles of Antrim. To die out of Ulster, when one can die in Ulster, there is a gey foolish thing . . ."

But the harsh logic of Ulster left me, and the soft mood of Ulster came on me, as I remembered him, and I going into the town on the train. And the late winter grass of Westchester, spare, scrofulous; the jerry-built bungalows; the lines of un-comely linen; the blatant advertising

boards—all the unbeauty of it passed
away, and I was again in the Antrim glens.
There was the soft purple of the Irish
Channel, and there the soft, dim outline
of Scotland. There was the herring
school silver in the sun, and I could see it
from the crags where the surf boomed
like a drum. And underfoot was the
heather, the springy heather, the belled
and purple heather . . .

And there came to me again the vision
of the old man's thatched farmhouse when
the moon was up and the bats were out,
and the winds of the County Antrim came
bellying down the glens . . . The turf fire
burned on the hearth, now red, now yel-
low, and there was the golden light of
lamps, and Malachi of the Long Glen was
reciting some poem of Blind Raftery's,
or the lament of Pierre Ronsard for
Mary, Queen of Scots:

*Ta ribin o mo cheadshearc ann mo phoca sios.*
*Agas mna Eirip ni leigheasfadaois mo bhron,*
 *faraor!*

*Ta me reidh leat go ndeantar damh comhra caol!*
*Agas gobhfasfaidh an fear no dhiaidh sin thrid mo*
*    lar anios!*

There is a ribbon from my only love in my pocket
    deep,
And the women of Europe they could not cure my
    grief, alas!
I am done with you until a narrow coffin be made
    for me.
And until the grass shall grow after that up
    through my heart!

And I suddenly discovered on the rum-
bling train that apart from the hurling and
the foot-ball and the jumping of horses,
what life I remembered of Ulster was
bound up in Malachi Campbell of the Long
Glen . . .

A very strange old man, hardy as a
blackthorn, immense, bowed shoulders,
the face of some old hawk of the mountains, hair white and plentiful as some old
cardinal's. All his kinsfolk were dead
except for one granddaughter . . . And
he had become a tradition in the glens . . .
It was said he had been an ecclesiastical
student abroad, in Valladolid, . . and that

he had forsaken that life. And in France he had been a tutor in the family of Mac-Mahon, *roi d' Irlande,* . . and somewhere he had married, and his wife had died and left him money, . . and he had come back to Antrim . . . He had been in the Papal Zouaves, and fought also in the American Civil War. . . A strange old figure who knew Greek and Latin as well as most professors, and who had never forgotten his Gaelic . . .

Antrim will ever color my own writing. My Fifth Avenue will have something in it of the heather glen. My people will have always a phrase, a thought, a flash of Scots-Irish mysticism, and for that I must either thank or blame Malachi Campbell of the Long Glen. The stories I heard, and I young, were not of Little Rollo and Sir Walter Scott's, but the horrible tale of the Naked Hangman, who goes through the Valleys on Midsummer's Eve; of Dermot, and Granye of the

Bright Breasts; of the Cattle Raid of
Maeve, Queen of Connacht; of the old
age of Cuchulain in the Island of Skye;
grisly, homely stories, such as yon of the
ghostly foot-ballers of Cushendun, whose
ball is a skull, and whose goal is the por-
tals of a ruined graveyard; strange religious poems, like the Dialogue of Death
and the Sinner:

Do thugainn loistin do gach deoraidh treith-lag—
I used to give lodging to every poor wanderer;
Food and drink to him I would see in want,
His proper payment to the man requesting reck-
    oning,
Och!  Is not Jesus hard if he condemns me!

All these stories, of all these people he
told, had the unreal, shimmering quality
of that mirage that is seen from Portrush
cliffs, a glittering city in a golden desert,
surrounded by a strange sea mist.  All
these songs, all these words he spoke, were
native, had the same tang as the turf
smoke, the Gaelic quality that is in dark
lakes on mountains summits, in plovers

nests amid the heather . . . And to remember them now in New York, to see
him . . .

Fifteen years had changed him but little:
a little more tremor and slowness in the
walk, a bow to the great shoulders, an eye
that flashed like a knife.

"And what do you think of New York,
Malachi?"

"I was here before, your honor will remember. I fought at the Wilderness."

I forbore asking him what change he
had found. I saw his quivering nostrils.

In a few days he would proceed south,
when he had orientated himself after the
days of shipboard.

That night it seemed every one chose
to come in and cluster around the fire.
Randall, the poet; and the two blond Dan-
ish girls, with their hair like flax; Fraser,
the golfer, just over from Prestwick; and
a young writer, with his spurs yet to win;
and this one . . . and that one.

They all kept silence as old Malachi spoke, sportsmen, artists, men and women of the world; a hush came on them, and their eyes showed they were not before the crackling fire in the long room, but amazed in the Antrim glens.

Yes, old Malachi said, things were changed over there, and a greater change was liable . . . People whispered that in the Valley of the Black Pig the Boar without Bristles had been seen at the close of the day, and in Templemore there was a bleeding image, and these were ominous portents . . . Some folks believed and some did n't . . . And the great Irish hunter that had won the Grand National, the greatest horse in the world . . . But our Man of War, Malachi? . . Oh, sure, all he could do was run, and a hare or a greyhound could beat him at that; but Shawn Spadah, a great jumper him, as well as a runner; in fine, a horse. . . And did I know that Red Simon McEwer of

Cushundall had gone around Portrush in eighteen consecutive fours? . . A Rathlin Islander had tried the swim across to Scotland, but did n't make it, and there was great arguing as to whether it was because of the currents or of lack of strength. . . There were rumblings in the Giants' Causeway . . . very strange . . . A woman in Oran had the second sight, the most powerful gift of second sight in generations . . . There was a new piper in Islay, and it was said he was a second McCrimmon . . . And a new poet had arisen in Uist, and all over the Highlands they were reciting his songs and his "Lament for the Bruce." . . Was I still as keen for, did I still remember the poems, and the great stories? . .

" 'Behold, the night is of great length,' " I quoted, " 'Unbearable. Tell us, therefore, of those wondrous deeds.' "

"If you 've remembered your Gaidhlig as you 've remembered your Greek!"

"It's a long time since you've had a story of me, twelve long years, and it's a long time before you'll have another, and I going away to-morrow. Old Sergeant Death has his warrant out for me this many a day, and it's only the wisdom of an old dog fox that eludes him; but he'll lay me by the heels one of these days, . . then there'll be an end to the grand stories . . . So after this, if you're wanting a story, you must be writing it yourself . . .

"But before I die, I'll leave you the story of Marco Polo. There's been a power of books written about Marco Polo. The scholars have pushed up their spectacles and brushed the cobwebs from their ears, and they've said, 'There's all there is about Marco Polo.'

"But the scholars are a queer and blind people, Brian Oge. I've heard tell there's a doctor in Spain can weigh the earth. But he can't plow a furrow that is needful

for planting corn. The scholars can tell
how many are the feathers in a bird's
wing, but it takes me to inform the doctors
why the call comes to them, and they fly
over oceans without compass or sextant
or sight of land.

"Did you ever see a scholar standing in
front of a slip of a girl? In all his learning he can find nothing to say to her. And
every penny poet in the country knows.

"Let you be listening now, Brian Oge,
and let also the scholars be listening. But
whether the scholars do or not, I'm not
caring. A pope once listened to me with
great respect, and a marshal of France
and poets without number. But the scholars do be turning up their noses. And,
mind you, I've got as much scholarship
as the next man, as you'll see from my
story.

"Barring myself, is there no one in
this house that takes snuff? No! Ah,
well, times do be changing."

# 1

NOW it 's nearing night on the first day of spring, and you could see how loath day was to be going for even the short time until the rising of the sun again. And though there was a chill on the canals, yet there was great color to the sunset, the red of it on the water ebbing into orange, and then to purple, and losing itself in the olive pools near the mooring-ties. And a little wind came up from the Greek islands, and now surged and fluttered, the way you 'd think a harper might be playing. You 'd hear no sound, but the melody was there. It was the rhythm of spring, that the old people recognize.

But the young people would know it was spring, too, by token of the gaiety that was in the air. For nothing brings joy

to the heart like the coming of spring.
The folk who do be blind all the rest of
the year, their eyes do open then, and a
sunset takes them, and the wee virgin flowers coming up between the stones, or the
twitter of a bird upon the bough . . . And
young women do be preening themselves,
and young men do be singing, even they
that have the voices of rooks.   There is
something stirring in them that is stirring
in the ground, with the bursting of the
seeds . . .

And young Marco Polo threw down the
quill in the counting house where he was
learning his trade.   The night was coming on.   He was only a strip of a lad, and
to lads the night is not rest from work,
and the quietness of sleeping, but gaming
and drinking, and courting young women.
Now, there were two women he might
have gone to, and one was a great Venetian lady, with hair the red of a queen's
cloak, and a great noble shape to her and

great dignity. But with her he would
only be reciting verses or making grand,
stilted compliments, the like of those you
would hear in a play. And while that
seemed to fit in with winter and candle-
light, it was poor sport for spring. The
other one was a black, plump little gown-
maker, a pleasant, singing little woman,
very affectionate, and very proud to have
one of the great Polos loving her. She
was eager for kissing, and always asking
the lad to be careful of himself, to be put-
ting his cloak on, or to be sure and drink
something warm when he got home that
night, for the air from the canals was
chill. The great lady was too much of the
mind, and the little gown-maker was too
much of the body, either of them, to be
pleasing young Marco on the first night
of spring.

Now, it is a queer thing will be pleasing
a young man on the first night of spring.
The wandering foot itches, and the mind

and body are keen to follow. There is that inside a young man that makes the hunting dog rise from the hearth on a moonlight night: "Begor! it's myself 'll take a turn through the fields on the chance of a bit of coursing. A weasel, maybe, or an otter, would be out the night. Or a hare itself. Ay, there would be sport for you! The hare running hell-for-leather, and me after him over brake and dell. Ay! Ay! Ay! a good hunt's a jewel! I'll take a stretch along the road."

Or there is in him what does be troubling the birds, and they on tropic islands. "Tweet-tweet," they grumble. "A grand place this surely, and very comfortable for the winter. The palm-trees are green, but I'd rather have the green of young grass. And the sea, you ken, it becomes monotonous. Do you remember the peaches of Champagne, wife, and the cherry-trees of Antrim? Do you remember the farmer who was such a bad shot, and his wife with the red petticoat? I'm feeling fine and strong in the wings, *avourneen*. What do you say? Let's bundle and go!"

He wandered out with the discontent of the season on him. The sun had dropped at last, and everywhere you'd see torches, and the image of torches in the water. On the canals of the town great barges moved. Everywhere were fine, noble shadows and the splashing of oars. There was a great admiral's galley, ready to put to sea against Genoa. There a big merchantman back from Africa. And along the canals went all the people in the world, you'd think. Now it was a Frenchman, all silks and satins and *"la-di-da, monsieur!"* Or a Spaniard with a pointed beard and long, lean legs and a long, lean sword. And now it was a Greek courtesan, white as milk, sitting in her gondola as on a throne. Here was a Muscovite, hairy, dirty, with fine fur and fine jewels and teeth sharp as a dog's. And now an effeminate Greek nobleman, languid as a bride. And here were Moorish captains, *Othello's* men, great giants of black marble; and swarthy, hook-nosed merchants of Palestine; and the squires of Crusaders—pretty, ringleted boys, swearing like demons. And here and there were Scots and Irish mercenaries, kilted, sensitive folk, one moment smiling at you and the next a knife in your gizzard.

And as he went through the courts there were whispers and laughter, and occasionally a soft voice invited him to enter; but he smiled and shook his head.

Near the Canal de Mestre, which is close by the Ghetto, he stopped by the wine-shop called The Prince of Bulgaria, and he could hear great disputation. And some were speaking of Baldwin II, and how he had no guts to have let Palæologus take Constantinople from him. And others were murmuring about Genoa.

"Mark us, they mean trouble, those dogs. Better wipe them off the face of the earth now." And a group were discussing the chances of raiding the Jewish Kingdom of the Yemen. "They 've got temples there roofed with gold." . . And an Irish piper was playing on a little silver set of pipes, and an Indian magician was doing great sleight of hand . . .

"I 'll go in and talk to the strange foreign people," said Marco Polo.

## II

NOW, you might be thinking that the picture I'm drawing is out of my own head. Let you not be thinking of it as it is now, a city of shadows and ghosts, with a few scant visitors mooning in the canals. The Pride of the West she was, the Jewel of the East. Constantinople was her courtyard. Greece, Egypt, Abyssinia, Bulgaria, and Muscovy, her ten-acre fields. The Crusaders on their way to fight the Saracen stopped to plead for her help and generosity. There were no soldiers more chivalrous, not even the French. There were no better fighters, not even the Highland clans. Sailors? You'd think those fellows had invented the sea. And as for riches and treasures, oh! the wonder of the world she was! Tribute she had from everywhere; the four great horses of Saint Mark they came from Constantinople. The two great marble columns facing the Piazetta, sure, they came from Acre. When foreign powers wanted the loan of money, it was to Venice they came. Consider the probity of Venetian men. They once held as pledge the Crown of Thorns itself. King Louis IX of France redeemed it.

The processions of the tradespeople were like a king's retinue, and they marching in state on the election of a doge. Each in their separate order they 'd come, the master smiths first, as is right, every one garlanded like a conqueror, with their banner and their buglers. The furriers next in ermine and taffeta; the tanners, with silver cups filled with wine; the tailors in white, with vermilion stars; the woolworkers, with olive branches; the quiltmakers in cloaks trimmed with fleur-de-lis; the cloth-of-gold weavers, with golden crowns set with pearls; the shoemakers

in fine silk, while the silk-workers were in
fustian; the cheese-dealers and pork-butch-
ers in scarlet and purple; the fish-mongers
and poulterers, armed like men-of-war;
the glass-makers, with elegant specimens
of their art; the comb-makers, with little
birds in cages; the barber-surgeons on
horseback, very dignified, very learned,
and with that you'd think there'd be an
end to them, but cast your eye back on that
procession and you'd find guilds as far
as your sight would reach . . .

Let you be going down the markets,
and what would you see for sale? Boots,
clothes, bread? No, they were out of
sight; but scattered on the booths, the
like of farls of bread on a fair-day, you'd
find cloves and nutmegs, mace and ebony
from Moluccas, that had come by way
of Alexandria and the Syrian ports; san-
dalwood from Timor, in Asia; camphor
from Borneo. Sumatra and Java sent ben-
zoin to her markets. Cochin China sent

bitter aloes-wood. From China and Japan and from Siam came gum, spices, silks, chessmen, and curiosities for the parlor. Rubies from Peru, fine cloths from Coromandel, and finer still from Bengal. They got spikenard from Nepaul and Bhutan. Their diamonds were from Golconda. From Nirmul they purchased Damascus steel for their swords. Nor is that all you 'd see, and you 'd be going down by the markets on a sunny morning, and a fine-thinking, low-voiced woman on your arm. You 'd see pearls and sapphires, topaz and cinnamon from Ceylon; lac and agates, brocades and coral from Cambay; hammered vessels and inlaid weapons and embroidered shawls from Cashmere. As for spices, never would your nostrils meet such an odor: bdellium from Scinde, musk from Tibet, galbanum from Khorasan; from Afghanistan, asafetida; from Persia, sagapenum; ambergris and civet from Zanzibar, and from Zanzibar came ivory, too. And from Zeila, Berbera, and Shehri came balsam and frankincense . . .

And that was Venice, and Marco Polo a young man. And now it 's only a town like any other town but for its churches and canals. There 's many a town has ghosts, but none the ghosts that Venice has; not Rome itself, or Tara of the kings.

"Once did she hold," Randall quoted, "the gorgeous
        East in fee;
And was the safeguard of the West; the worth
Of Venice did not fall below her birth,
Venice, the eldest Child of Liberty.
She was a maiden city, bright and free;
No guile seduced, no force could violate;
And, when she took unto herself a mate,
She must espouse the everlasting Sea!"

Time is the greatest rogue of all. Not all the arrows of Attila can do the damage of a trickle of sand in an hour-glass! Tyre and Sidon, Carthage, ancient Babylon, and Venice, queen of them all.

I am describing Venice to you for this reason. You might now stand where

Troy's walls once were and say to yourself: "Was this where Helen walked with
her little son? Was this where the love-
liest face of ages wept?" And a chill of
doubt would come on you, and you would
think, "I 've been wasting my sorrow and
wasting my love, for it was all nothing
but an old tale made up in a minstrel's
head."

And sometime in Venice, after your din-
ner in a hotel, you 'd go out for a while
in a *barca*, that would have no more ro-
mance to it nor the bark a gillie would row,
and you salmon-fishing on a cold, blus-
tery day, and you would feel disappointed,
you having come so far, and you 'd say:
"It was a grand story surely, and bravely
did it pass the winter evening; but was n't
old Malachi of the Long Glen the liar of
the world!"

I wouldn 't have you saying that, and
I dead. In all I 'm telling you, I 'd have
you to know there 's not a ha'porth of lie.

# III

AND so Marco Polo went into the wine-shop to see and hear the strange foreign people.

It was a dark, long room, very high, full of shadows between the flaming torches on the wall. At one side of it was a great fire burning, for all it was the first night of spring. At one end of it were the great barrels of liquor for the thirsty customers; black beer for the English and the Irish, grand, hairy stuff with great foam to it, and brown beer for the Germans; and there was white wine there for the French people, and red wine for the Italians, asquebaugh for the Scots, and rum from the sugar cane for such as had cold in their bones. There was all kind of drink there in the brass-bound barrels—drink would make you mad and

drink would make you merry, drink
would put heart in a timid man and
drink would make fighting men peaceful as
pigeons; and drink that would make you
forget trouble—all in the brass-bound barrels at the end of the room. And pleasant,
fat little men were roaming around serv-
ing the varied liquor in little silver cups,
and fine Venetian glasses for the wine,
and in broad-bellied drinking-pots that
would hold more than a quart.

And there was such a babel of language
as was never heard but in one place before.

Some of the drinkers were dicing and
shouting as they won, and grumbling and
cursing when they lost. And some were
singing. And some were dancing to the
Irish pipes. And there was a knot around
the Indian conjurer.

But there was one man by himself at a
table. And him being so silent, you'd
think he was shouting for attention. He
was so restful against the great commo-

tion, you'd know he was a great man. You might turn your back on him, and you'd know he was there, though he never even whispered nor put out a finger. A fat, pleasant, close-coupled man he was, in loose, green clothes, with gold brocade on them. And there were two big gold ear-rings in his lobes. He smoked a wee pipe with the bowl half-ways up it. The pipe was silver and all stem, and the bowl no bigger than a ten-cent piece. His shoulders were very powerful, so you'd know he was a man you should be polite to, and out of that chest of his a great shout could come. He might have been a working-man, only, when he fingered his pipe, you'd see his hands were as well kept as a lord's lady's, fine as silk and polished to a degree. And you'd think maybe a pleasant poet, which is a scarce thing, until you looked at the brown face of him and big gold ear-rings. And then you'd

know what he was: he was a great sea-
captain.

But where did he come from? You
might know from the high cheek bones
and the eyes that were on a slant, as it
were, that it was an Eastern man was in
it. It might be Java and it might be
Borneo, or it might be the strange country
of Japan.

And there were a couple of strange oc-
currences in the wine-shop. The Indian
juggler was being baited by the fighting
men, as people will be after poking coarse
fun at a foreigner. The slim Hindu fellow was n't taking it at all well. He was
looking with eyes like gimlets at a big
bullock of a soldier that was leading the
tormenters.

"Show me something would surprise
me," he was ordering. "Be damned to
this old woman's entertainment!" says he.
"As a magician," says he, "you 're the

worst I ever saw. If you 're a magician,"
says he, "I 'm a rabbit."

And there was a roar at that, because
he was known to be a very brave man.

"Show me a magic trick," says he.

Says the Hindu:

"Maybe you 'd wish you had n't seen
it."

"Be damned to that!" says the big fellow.

"Look at this man well," the Hindu told
the room. "Look at him well." He
throws a handful of powder in the fire
and chants in his foreign language. A
cloud of white smoke arises from the fire.
He makes a pass before it, and, lo and
behold ye! it 's a screen against the wall.
And there 's a great commotion of shadows on the screen, and suddenly you see
what it 's all about. It 's a platform,
and a man kneeling, with his head on the
block. You don't see who it is, but you
get chilled. And suddenly there 's a heads-

man in a red cloak and a red mask, and
the ax swings and falls. The head pops
off, and the body falls limp. And the head
rolls down the platform and stops, and
you see it 's the head of the fellow who
wanted to see something, and it 's in the
grisly grin of death . . .

"There 's your latter end for you," says
the conjurer. "You wanted to see something. I hope you 're content."

The big fellow turns white, gulps, gives
a bellow, and makes a rush; but the conjurer is n't there, nor his screen nor anything.

Everybody in the room was white and
shaken—all but the sea-captain. He just
tamps his pipe as if nothing had happened, and smokes on. He does n't even
take a drink from his glass.

And a little while later an Irish chieftain walks in. He 's poor and ragged
and very thin. You might know he'd
been fighting the heathen for the Holy

Sepulchre, and so entitled to respect, no matter what his condition. And behind him are five clansmen as ragged as he. But a big German trooper rolls up.

"And what are you?" says the big, burly fellow.

"A gentleman, I hope," says the ragged chief.

" 'Tis yourself that says it," laughs the German trooper. The chieftain snicks the knife from his armpit, and sticks him in the jugular as neat as be damned.

"You 'd might take that out, Kevin Beg"—the Irish chief points to the killed man—"and throw it in the canal. Somebody might stumble over it and bark their shins."

Now this, as you can conceive, roused a powerful commotion in the room. They were all on their feet, captains and mariners and men-at-arms, cheering or grumbling, and arguing the rights and wrongs of the matter. All but the sea-captain, who saw it all, and he never blinked an eyelid, never even missed a draw of the pipe.

And then Marco Polo knew him to be a Chinaman, because, as all the world knows, Chinamen are never surprised at anything.

# IV

SO Marco Polo goes over and salutes him politely.

"I wonder if you mind my sitting down by you for a while," he says. "I perceive you 're from China."

The sea-captain waves him politely to his place.

"I 'm from China." He smiles. "You guessed right."

"Is it long since you 've been in China?"

"Well, that depends upon what you call long," says the captain. "If you mean time, it 's one thing. If you mean voyage, it 's another. For you 've got to take into account," says he, "adverse winds, roundabout turns to avoid currents, possible delays to have the ship scraped free from the parasite life that does be attaching itself to the strakes, time spent in

barter and trade.   Other matters, too;
the attacks of pirates; cross-grained princes who don't want you to be leaving their
ports with a good cargo in your hold;
sickness; loss of sails and masts; repairs
to the ship.   It was n't a short journey
and it was n't a long one."

"It will be a long ways to China, I 'm
thinking."

"I can tell you how long it is from
China to here, and you can reverse that,
and you will get a fair idea of how long
it is from here to China.   I left Zeitoon
with a cargo of porcelain for Japan, and
traded it for gold-dust, and from Japan
I went to Chamba to lay in a store of
chessmen and pen-cases. And from Chamba I sailed to Java, which is the greatest
island in the world.   Java is fifteen hundred miles from Chamba, south and south-
east, and it took me four months sailing,
but a sea-captain cannot pass Java by, for
it is the chief place for black pepper, nut-

megs, spikenard, galingale, cubebs, cloves, and all the spices that grow.

"And I stopped at various small islands from there, until I came to Basma, which is the island of the unicorns. And there we trade in pygmies, which ignorant people think are human folk. They are just a wee monkey, with all the hair plucked out except the hair of the beard. There is great money in them.

"I stopped at Sumatra for cocoanuts and toddy, and just for water at Dragoian. Dragoian is not a good city. It is filled with sorcerers who have tattooed faces. At Lambri I put in for the sago you buy from the hairy men with tails.

"Son, never stop at the isle of Andaman. The men there have faces like dogs. They are a cruel generation, and eat every one they can catch. I could tell you a story, but I would not spoil this fine spring night. Go rather to the island of Ceylon, and see the King's Ruby, which is the greatest jewel in the world. I stopped there and at Coromandel for the pearls the divers go down in the sea for, and there are no clothes on that island, so that every one goes naked as a fish. And there is the shrine of Saint Thomas. I was there.

"Gujarat, Tana, I stopped there. The Male and Female Islands I put into for ambergris. Svestra, which is full of magicians—I was there, too. Madagascar and Zanzibar, where they live on camel flesh, I was there. And from Zanzibar I came north to Abyssinia, because I had to get an ostrich there for the King of Siam. And there was a letter and a parcel for the Sultan of Egypt. So I went to Cairo. I had a month on my hands, so I thought I'd run over and see Venice, because it's a hobby of mine, you might say, to see the world.

"Now let me reckon. Four and three makes seven, and four more are eleven,

and six are seventeen, and let us say nine
with that, and you have twenty-six. And
the month I'm forgettng on the rocks of
Aden is twenty-seven, and a week here
and a week there for bad winds and such
like. It would be safe to put that at three
months. So it's two years and a half since
I left China."

"You never," says young Marco, "met
anybody in China by the name of Polo?"

"Poh-lo? Poh-lo? China's a bigger
place nor you would imagine, laddie.
There's half a hundred million people
there."

"These were foreigners," Marco ex-
plained, "traders. They were at the court
of the great Khan."

"Polo? Polo? Well, now, I think
I've heard of them. Was one of them a
big red-bearded man with a great eye for
a horse and a great eye for a woman?"

"That would be my Uncle Matthew."

"For God's sake! And was the other

a cold, dark man, a good judge of a jewel and a grand judge of a sword?"

"My father, Nicholas Polo."

"For God's sake! you're the son of one and the nephew of the other!"

"Did you know them?"

"Ah, laddie, how would I be knowing people like that! Sure, they're great folks, high in the esteem of the grand Khan, and I'm only a poor sailorman."

"But you heard of them."

"I heard of them. They were in good health. And I heard they were on their way home, though they would travel overland and not risk the great dangers of the sea. I suppose, if they go back to China, you'll be going with them?"

"I don't know," says Marco Polo.

"You ought to see China. It's a great country, a beautiful country."

"It would have to be very great and beautiful," says Marco Polo, "to outweigh the greatness and the beauty that are here. You must n't think I 'm running down your country, mister," says he; "but for greatness, where is the beating of Venice in this day? What struck Constantinople like a thunderbolt but the mailed hand of Venice? When the Barbary corsairs roamed the seven seas, so that it was no more safe for a merchant vessel to be sailing than for a babe to be walking through a wild jungle, it was Venice who accepted the challenge and made the great sea as peaceful as the Grand Canal. Who humbled proud Genoa? And hurled the Saracen from Saint John of Acre's walls? Venice. And as for magnificence, the retinue of our doge when he goes to marry the sea with a ring it makes the court of Lorenzo seem like a huckster's train."

"It is a crowning city."

"And as for beauty, sir," went on Marco Polo, "there is nothing in the world like San Marco's, and it ablaze in the setting sun, and the great pillars before it rising in tongues of flame. And was there ever in all time anything like the Grand Canal at the dusk of day, and the torches beginning to show like fireflies, and the lap of the water, and stringed music, and the great barges going by like swans, now a battle-hacked captain of war, now a great gracious lady? And the moon does be rising . . .

"You 've sailed all the way from China and seen strange and beautiful things, but I remember one summer's day, when I took out my little sailing-boat and went out on the water to compose a poem for a lady, and the water was blue—oh, as blue as the sky's self, and the sands of the Lido were silver, and the water shuffled gently over them, as gently as a child's little feet. And there was a clump of olive-trees there so green as to be black, and there alighted before it a great scarlet Egyptian bird. And the beauty of that brought the tears to my eyes, so that

I thought of nuns in their cells and barefoot friars in the hollow lands, and they striving for paradise. What did I care about paradise? A Venetian I. So why should I want to go to China?"

"You have made a great case for the grandeur and beauty of Venice," says the sea-captain. "It is lovely, surely," says he, filling his pipe; "but finer poets nor you, my lad," says he, lighting it, "have tried to describe the grace and beauty of Tao-Tuen, and," says he taking a draw, "have failed."

"Tao-Tuen is a beautiful name. It is like two notes plucked on a harp. And it must be a wonderful place, surely, if great poets cannot describe it."

"It is not a place," said the captain, "it 's a girl."

"As for women, Venice—"

"Venice be damned!" said the sea-captain. "Not in Venice, not in all the world, is there the like for grace or beauty of

Tao-Tuen. They call her Golden Bells,"
he says.

"Is she a dancing-girl?" Marco asked.

"She is not a dancing-girl," says the sea-
captain, "she is the daughter of Kubla,
the great Khan."

"A cold and beautiful princess," says
Marco Polo.

"She is not a cold and beautiful princess," says the sea-captain. "She is warm
as the sun in early June, and she may be
beautiful and a princess, but we all think
of her as Golden Bells, the little girl in
the Chinese garden."

"Did you ever see her?" says Marco,
eagerly. "Tell me."

"I saw her before I left," says the sea-
captain. "I was at the Khan's palace of
Chagannor," says he, "seeing of the chief
of the stewards was there anything I could
get for him, and I in foreign parts. And
as I was being rowed back along the river

by my ten brawny sailormen, what did I pass but the garden of Golden Bells.

"And there she was by the river-side, a little brown slip of a girl in green coat and trousers, with a flower in her dark hair.

"And I lower my head in reverence as we pass by. But I hear her low, merry voice, by reason of which they call her Golden Bells.

" 'Ho, master of the vessel!' she calls. 'Where do you go?'

"And the sailors back water with a swish, and I stand up respectfully, for all she is only a slip of a girl.

" 'I go to foreign parts, Golden Bells,' I tell her; 'to far and dangerous places, into the Indian Ocean. To the Island of Unicorns and to the land where men eat men.'

" 'I hope you come back safe, master of the vessel,' she says. 'I hope you have a good voyage and come back safe. It must be a dreadful strain on your people to think of you so far away.'

" 'In all this wide land,' I tell her, 'there is none to worry about me. I have neither chick nor child.'

" 'Golden Bells will worry about you, then,' she said, 'and you in the hazards of the sea. And take this flower for luck.' And she gave me the flower from her hair. 'And let it bring you luck against the anger of the ocean and the enemies all men have. And let me know when you are back, because I 'll be worried about a man of China and him in danger on the open sea.'

"And was n't that a wonderful thing from a daughter of Kubla to me, a poor sailor-man?

"The son of the King of Siam came to woo her with a hundred princes on a hundred elephants, but she would n't have him. 'I don't wish to be a queen,' she told her father. 'How could I be a

queen? I am only Golden Bells.' Nor
would she have anything to say to the
Prince of the Land of Darkness, who came
to her with sea ivory and pale Arctic gold.
'The sun of China is in my heart, and you
would n't have me go up into the great
coldness to shiver and die?'

"So she remains in her garden by the
lake of Cranes with Li Po, the great poet,
him they call the Drinker of Wine, to
make songs for her; and the *Sanang* Tung.
Chih, the great magician, to perform
wonders for her when she is wearied; and
Bulagan, her nurse, to take her to her
heart when she is sad.

"And sad she is a lot of the time, they
tell me. She sits in her garden in the
dusk, playing her lute, and singing the
song of the Willow branches, which is the
saddest love-song in the world . . .

"And why she should be singing a sad
love-song, is a mystery, for her soft, brown
beauty is the flower of the world. For

there would be no lack of suitors for her, nor is she the one to refuse love. The only thing I make of it is that the right hour has n't come.

"The beauty of Venice jumps to your eyes, but the beauty of this pulls at your heart. Little brown Golden Bells, in her Chinese garden, singing the song of the Willow Branches at the close of day . . . Is that not better nor Venice?"

But he got no word out of Marco Polo, sitting with his chin cupped in his hands. And that was the finest answer at all, at all.

## V

THE times went by, and Marco Polo busied himself with his daily affairs, keeping track of the galleasses with merchandise to strange far-away ports, buying presents for refractory governors who did n't care for foreign trade in their domains, getting wisdom from the old clerks, and knowledge from the mariners; in the main, acting as the son of a great house while the heads of it were away.

You would think that he would have forgotten what the sea-captain of China told him about Golden Bells, what with work and sport and other women near him. You would think that would drop out of his memory like an old rime. But it stuck there, as an old rime sometimes sticks, and by dint of thinking he had her fast now in his mind—so fast, so clear,

so full of life, that she might be some one
he had seen an hour ago or was going to
see an hour from now.   He would think
of the now merry, now sad eyes of her,
and the soft, sweet voice of her by reason
of which they called her Golden Bells, and
the dusky little face, and the hair like
black silk, and the splotch of the red
flower in it.   She was as distinct to him as
the five fingers on his hand.   It was n't
only she was clear in his mind's eye, but
she was inside of him, closer than his
heart.   She was there when the sun rose,
so he would be saying, "It 's a grand day is
in it surely, Golden Bells."   She was there
in the dim counting house and he going
over in the great intricate ledgers the
clerks do be posting carefully with quills
of the gray goose, so that he would be
saying:   "I wonder where this is and
that is.   Sure I had my finger on it only
a moment ago, Golden Bells."   And when
the dusk was falling, and the bats came

out, and the quiet of Christ was over
everything, and the swallows flew low on
the great canals, she would be beside him,
and never a word would he say to her, so
near to him would she be.

And she wrought strangeness between
him and the women he knew, the great
grave lady with the large, pale mouth, her
that was of his mind, and the little black
cloak-maker with the eager, red mouth,
her that was closer than mind or heart to
him. So that the first found fault with his
poetry.

"I do n't know what 's come over you,
Marco Polo,"—and there was a touch
of temper in her voice,—"but these poems
of yours show me you have n't your mind
on your subject. Would you mind telling
me when I had bound black hair?" she
says. "And you say my bosom is like two
little russet apples. Now, a regular poet
once compared it to two great silver cups,
and that was a good comparison, though

in truth," she says, "he knew as little about it as you. And my hands are not like soft Eastern flowers. They're like lilies. I don't know where you do be getting these Eastern comparisons," she says. "But I don't like them. Tell me, pretty boy,"— she looks suspicious,—"you haven't been taking any of the strange Egyptian drugs the dark people do be selling in the dim shops on the quiet canals? Look out, pretty boy! look out!"

And the little cloak-maker grumbled when he was gone. "I don't know what's wrong with him," says she. "Or maybe it's something that's wrong with myself, but this delicate love isn't a'l it's cracked up to be. It's all right in books," she says, "and it's a grand sight, and the players doing it; but I like a hug," she says, "would put the breath out of you; and a kiss," she says, "you could feel in the soles of your feet." And she lay awake and grumbled. "Let him be taking his la-di-da courting to those as favor it," says she. "It's not my kind," and she grumbled through the lonely night. "I wonder where my husband is now," she said. "And was n't I the foolish girl to be sending him off! Sure, he drank like a fish and beat me something cruel, but he was a rare lover, and the mood on him. Sure, a woman never knows when she's well off," says she.

And Marco Polo did n't miss them any more nor you'd miss an old overcoat and the winter past. All his mind was on was the Golden Bells of China. And he thought long until his uncle and father came, so that he could be off with them to the strange Chinese land.

"But there's no use to me going there," says he. "I could n't marry her. She would laugh at me," he says. "She, who refused the son of the King of Siam, with his hundred princes on a hundred elephants, what use would she have for

me, who's no better nor a pedler with his
pack? But it would be worth walking the
world barefoot for to see that little golden face, to hear the low, sweet voice they
call Golden Bells."

They came back in due time, his uncle
Matthew, the red, hairy man, and his
father, the thin, dark man, who knew precious stones. And he told them he wanted
to go with them when they made their
next expedition to China.

"We could be using you, after your
training in trade," says the father. But
Marco Polo would take no interest in
barter. "Sure, you'd better come along,"
says his uncle Matthew. "There's great
sport to be had on the road, kissing and
courting the foreign women and not a
word of language between you, barring a
smile and a laugh."

"I have no interest in the foreign women, Uncle Matthew."

"Then it's the horses you've been hearing about, the fine Arab horses faster nor the wind, and the little Persian ponies they do be playing polo on, and the grand Tatar hunters that can jump the heighth of a man, and they sure-footed as a goat. Ah, the horses, the bonny horses!"

"Ah, sure, Uncle Matthew, 't is little I know of horses. Sure, I know all about boats, racing and trade and war boats, but a horse is not kin to me."

"Then what the hell's the use of your going to China?"

"Ah, sure, that's the question I'm asking myself, Uncle Matthew. But I have to go. I do so. There is something calling me, Uncle Matthew—a bell in my ear, father's brother, and there's a ringing bell in my heart."

# VI

I SHALL now tell you how it came about that Marco Polo went to China with his uncle and father, though he had no eye for a bargain, or interest in courting foreign women, or sense of horses.

Now, as you may know, this was a great religious time. The Crusaders, feeling shame that the Sepulchre of the Lord Jesus should be in Saracen hands, had come with horse, foot and artillery to Palestine to give tribute of arms to Him who had died for them on the Bitter Tree. And great feats were performed and grand battles won. And kings became saints, like Louis of France, and saints became kings, like Baldwin of Constantinople. Mighty wonders were seen and miracles performed, so that people said, "Now

will be the second coming of Christ and
the end of the world."

And a great desire came on the Christian people to tell the truth of Christ to
the strange and foreign peoples of the
world.  So that every day out of Jerusalem you would see friars hitting the road,
some of them to confront the wizards of
the Land of Darkness, and some to argue
theology with the old lamas of Tibet, and
some to convert the sunny Southern
islands, where the young women do be
letting down their hair and the men do
be forgetting God for them.  And all over
the world there was spreading a great
rumor that the truth of all things was at
last known.

Even Kubla Khan had heard of it far
off in China, and he had charged the uncle
and father of Marco with a message to
the Pope of Rome.  Let the pope be sending some theologians to his court, and
they 'd argue the matter out; and if he was

satisfied that this new religion was the
True Religion, then he 'd turn Christian
and tell his people to turn Christian, too.
And let them be bringing back some of the
Oil of the Lamp which burns in the Holy
Sepulchre at Jerusalem and is a cure for
all the ills in the world.

And when they came to the City of
Acre, sure the pope was dead. And they
waited a long time, but no new pope was
chosen, so they decided to go back, because they had a good business there, and
they did n't want to lose it. And yet they
knew there 'd be trouble with the Grand
Khan, if they did n't bring back the news
of the True Religion and people to argue
it.

"I 've been a long time trading," says
Nicolo, "and it 's a queer thing, but the
more trading you do, the less religion you
have. The arguing of religion would not
come easy to me. And I 'd be up against

experts. I'm not the man for it," says he. "How about you, Matthew?"

"Oh, sure, they'd never listen to me," Matthew laughs—"me that's drank with them, and deludhered their women, and gambled until I left them nothing but the sweat of their brows. I'd be a great one to preach religion to them. Why, man, they'd laugh at me. But I tell you what, Nicolas. There's a bishop in Negropont, and I know where he lives, and I know his house and everything. What do you say, Nicolas? We'll just throw a bag over his head and tie him on a horse. Oh, sure, he'd give grand discourses to the Great Khan!"

"Have sense, Matthew; have sense. You're always too rough; always ready to end an argument with a knife, or just lift what you want. Have sense, man; you can't kidnap a bishop like you'd kidnap a woman."

"Well, I don't see why not," says Mat,

thew. "It would be easier, too, because a woman will scratch like a wildcat. But if you 're set against it, I won't do it,' he says. "Well, then, how about young Marco?"

"My sound man Matthew! my bully fellow! Sure you were never at a loss yet! Young Marco it is; sure, 't is the elegant idea. There 's not a man born of woman better for the job."

Now, all the Christian world had gone religious, and young Marco was no exception; for 't is not only the old that are religious. The young are, too; but there 's a difference. The religion of old men is reason and translation; the religion of the young is just a burning cloud. The Tragedy of the Bitter Tree is not a symbol to them, but a reality, and their tears are not of the spirit, but of the body, too.

And there are no half-way houses, no compromises, in a young man's creed. It 's swallow all, or be damned to you. It's believe or be lost.

And thinking over the little girl in the Chinese garden, there had come into Marco's heart, a thought past enduring. If little Golden Bells did not believe, then little Golden Bells was lost. She might have everything in this world, in this life, an emperor for a father, kings for suitors, a great poet for a minstrel, a wizard for an entertainer; but once the little blue shadow left her body, she was lost forever. And the sight came to him of little Golden Bells going down the dim and lonely alleys of death, and weeping, weeping, weeping . . . Her eyes would be shot with panic, and the little mouth twisted, and the little flowery hands twitching at each other. And it would be cold there for her who was so warm, and it would be dark there for her who loved light, and the Golden Bells of her voice would be lost in the whistling and clanging of the stars as they swung by in their orbits. He to be in the great delight of paradise, and she to be in the blue-gray maze between the worlds —what tragedy!

Kings might bring her presents, a husband might bring her happiness; but if he could only bring her salvation! If he could only tell her of the Bitter Tree!

The body, when you came to think of it, mattered little. All the beauty in the world could not endure more than its appointed span. Helen was dust now, and Deirdre nothing. What had become of the beauty of Semiramis, Alexander's darling; and Cleopatra, who loved the great proconsul; and Bathsheba, for whom David of the Psalms fell from grace? And Balkis, queen of Sheba, with her apes, ivory, and peacocks? Dust and ashes, dust and ashes! And Scheherazade was but a strange, sad sound. Beauty increased and waned like the moon. A little shadow around the eyes, a little crinkle in the neck, the backs of the hands stiffening like parchment. Dust and ashes, dust and ashes!

But the little blue shadow would glow like an Easter morning.

Or it would be a poor, lonely, unlit shadow in the cold gloom of the clanging worlds.

Poor Golden Bells! Poor little weeping Golden Bells! If he could only tell her about the Bitter Tree!

And then what happens but his uncle Matthew claps him on the back.

"How would you like to go to China, Marco Markeen," says he, "and preach religion to the benighted people!"

"How did you know, Uncle Matthew?"

"How did I know what?"

"That I wanted to go to China and preach religion to the—the people!"

"Well, if that does n't beat Banagher," says Matthew Polo, "and Banagher beats the devil! Tell me, did you ever hear an old tune called 'Bundle and Go!'?"

And so the three of them leave upon their journey, but at Layas, where the King of Armenia had his castle, they heard of the election of a new pope, so they came back to Acre to get his instructions and blessing.

# VII

THE pope said a grand mass for them, and at the gospel he enters the pulpit, a burly figure of a man with sad eyes.

"The blessing of the Father and the Son and the Holy Ghost be with you and about you, Amen.

"It is not to you, Nicolo Polo, that I wish to speak, nor to you, Matthew Polo, for neither of you are my ambassadors to the Great Khan. Merchant and sportsman, I honor you, and you have my blessing, but you have no hopes of mine. The dirty diversions of the world are between your eyes and glory," said he. "It 's only myself, an old and sorrowful man, and this child, a young and hopeful one, can understand; old men having sight of visions, and young men dreaming dreams . . .

"Now in the matter of converting the

65

Great Khan and his numerous millions,
first let wisdom speak.  I have little hopes.
He wants to be argued into it, you see. Religion is not a matter of argument.  It is
a wisdom that surpasses wisdom.  It
drifts in men's souls as the foggy dew
comes unbidden to the trees.  It is born
before our soul, as the horned moon is
born before our eyes.

"And now, my child, you might say,
'What is the use of sending me to China
if he knows I cannot bring these millions
into the fold?'  My dear son, there is the
wisdom surpassing wisdom.  A great and
noble thought must not die.  Things of
the spirit we cannot reckon as a husband-
man reckons his crops.  There is a folk on
the marches of Europe, and they are ever
going into battle, and they always fall.
Their results are nothing.  But their name
and their glory wil. endure forever . . .

"My dear son, God has put wisdom in
my head and beauty into yours.  Wisdom

is needed for the governance of this world,
but beauty is needed for its existence. In
arid deserts there is no life. Birds do
not sing in the dark of night. Show me a
waste country, and I 'll show you a brutal
people. No faith can live that is not beautiful . . .

"The beauty God has put in your
heart, child, you must always keep . . .
How much I think of it I 'll tell you. I 'm
an old man now, an old and broken man,
and in a few years I 'll stand before my
Master.

" 'What have you seen on my earth,'
He 'll ask me, 'you who followed St.
Peter l'

" 'Lord! Lord l' I 'll tell Him, 'I've
seen mighty things. I 've seen the bride-
groom leave his bride and the king his
kingdom, the huckster leave his booth,
and the reaper drop his hook, that they
might rescue Your Holy Sepulchre from
pagan hands.'

"' 'And anything else?' He 'll ask.

"' 'And I 've seen a young man go out into the desert and over his head was a star. . .'

"You may think you have failed, child, but remember that in the coming times your name and fame will awaken beauty, and many 's the traveler on the hard road will find his courage again, and he thinking of Marco Polo. And many 's the young man will dream dreams, and many 's the old man will see visions, and they reading the book by the golden candle-light; and many 's the young girl will give you love, and you dead for centuries. But for this you must keep your dream.

"Now you 'll think it 's the queer pope I am to be telling you things like this instead of demanding converts. But the wisdom that surpasses wisdom comes to you with the Anointing of the Oil. 'I knew a man in Christ above fourteen years ago,' writes Saint Paul, '(whether in the body I cannot tell, or whether out of the body I cannot tell. God knoweth.)'

" 'How that he was caught up into paradise, and heard unspeakable words, which is not lawful for a man to utter.'

"Now you see there is a wisdom surpassing wisdom, and it is out of this fount of wisdom I am drawing when I speak to you these words.

"Child, I will not keep you any longer. Only to say this, and this is the chiefest thing: never let your dream be taken from you. Keep it unspotted from the world. In darkness and in tribulation it will go with you as a friend; but in wealth and power hold fast to it, for then is danger. Let not the mists of the world, the gay diversions, the little trifles, draw you from glory.

"Remember!

"*Si oblitus fuero tui Jerusalem,*—If I forget thee, O Jerusalem,—

"*Oblivioni detur dextera mea,*—let my right hand forget her cunning—

"*Adhaereat lingua mea faucibus meis, si non meminero tui,*—if I do not remember thee, let my tongue cleave to the roof of my mouth—

"*Si non proposuero Jerusalem, in principis laetitiæ meae,*—if I prefer not Jerusalem above my chief joy.

"I shall now send a prayer to Heaven," he said, "to keep you safe in the strange foreign ways, to protect you against wind and tempest, against pestilence and sudden death, against the powers of darkness, and Him who goes up and down the world for the ruin of souls."

And he turned to the high altar again, and now you'd hear his voice loud and powerful, and now low and secret, and the bell struck, and the acolyte intoned the responses, and all of a sudden he turned and spread forth his hands.

"*Ite!* Let you go now. *Missa est.*"

# VIII

AND so they set forth with their great
train of red, snarling camels and
little patient donkeys and slender, nervous
horses toward the rising sun. Behind
them the green hills of Palestine died out
as a rainbow dies out, and now there was
sand before them and now bleak mountains, and by day the wind was swift and
hot and by night it was black and cold.
And moons were born and died . . .

And they passed through the land of
the King of Armenia, and they passed
Ararat, the mountain where Noë brought
his ark to anchor, and where it still is,
and where it can be seen still, but cannot
be reached, so cold and high and terrible
is that mountain.

And they passed ruined Babel, that was
built of Nimrod, the first king of the

world, and now is desolation. They passed
it on a waning moon. And out of the ruins
the dragons came and hissed at them, and
strange, obscene birds flapped their wings
in the air and cawed and pecked at them,
and over the desert the satyr called unto
her mate. . .

And they passed through the Kingdom
of Georgia, whose kings are born with
the mark of an eagle on their right
shoulder. They passed through Persia,
where the magicians worship fire. And
they passed through the city of Saba,
where sleep the three magi who came to
worship at Bethlehem, and their names
were Kaspar, Balthasar, and Melchior.

And they passed through Camadi, where
great ruins are and robbers roam through
the magical darkness. And they passed
northward of the Perilous Valley, where
the Devil's Head is in black stone, and
that is one of the nine entrances to hell;
and passed the Valley of the Cockadrills,

where there are serpents five fathoms in
length; and passed the Valley of Cruel
Women, who have precious stones in
place of eyes . . .

And they went through the Dismal
Desert, where no stream sang . . .

And in the desert they passed the Trees
of the Sun and Moon, which speak with
the voices of men. And it was from the
Speaking Tree that Alexander heard of
his death. And it was near there that
he and Darius fought. And they passed
the *Arbre Sec,* the Dry Tree, which has
a green bark on one side and white on the
other, and there are no trees within a
hundred miles of that tree, and it is
sprung from the staff of Adam.

And they passed through Balkh, the
Mother of Cities. And they passed
through Taihan, where the great salt
mountains are. And they passed through
Badashan, where the mountains of the
rubies are. And they passed through

Kashmir, whose women are very beautiful, and whose magicians weave the strongest spells in the world . . .

And moons were born and died . . .

And they came to Alamoot, the fortress of *Senex de Monte,* the Old Man of the Mountain, the King of the Assasins, the greatest wizard of all time . . .

Now this is the tale of the Old Man of the Mountain.

Whenever within his dominions there was a fine young horseman, the Old Man would put a spell on him and draw him to the Castle of Alamoot, and outside of the castle sleep would come on him. And when he woke up, he would be inside the castle, in the wonderful gardens. And they 'd tell him he was dead and in paradise. And paradise it would be for him, what with the lovely women and the great playing on the flutes, the birds singing, and the sun shining, the crystal rivers and the flowers of the world. And after a while the Old Man of the Mountain would call for him, and tell him he was sending him back on earth again on a mission to punish Such-and-Such. And the Old Man would put sleep on him and a knife in his hand, and when he woke he would be outside the Castle of Alamoot. And he would start on his mission. And when he came back he would be readmitted to paradise. And if he did n't come back, there were others to take his place.

The Old Man of the Mountain always kept one hundred and one assasins and four hundred and four women to tend them.

Now when the caravan of the Polos had come to rest for the day, the Old Man of the Mountain put out white, not black magic, and he drew Marco Polo to the castle as a magnet draws a needle. And Marco Polo galloped up to the Castle in the waning moon, and the Old Man looked down on him from the battlements and stroked his long white beard.

"Do you know me, Marco Polo?"

"I know you and I have no fear of you, Old Man of the Mountain."

"And why have you no fear of me, Marco Polo?"

"Because the cross of the Lord Jesus is between me and harm. Because it protects me night and day."

"I know Eesa ben-Miriam," said the Old Man. "He was a great prophet. But whether he would have protected you from me, we will differ about that. I 've often thought of you, Marco Polo, and you coming this way. I could have used you in my work of keeping the kings and chieftains of the world in fear and subjection."

"Then why am n't I in your garden, Old Man of the Mountain?"

"The four most beautiful women in the world are in my garden. There is a tall,

black-haired woman, and she is fairer and
more adroit than Lilith, who was before
Eve; and there is a tall, blond woman,
and she is like a queen; and there is a
slim, copper-colored woman, and she is
like an idol in a shrine; and there is a little
brown-haired woman, and she is like a
child.   But none of those women could
make you believe you were in paradise
while there 's a face in your heart.   Not
the cross of the Lord Jesus is between you
and me, but the face of little Golden Bells
of China."

"But I am not going to China to woo
Golden Bells, Old Man of the Mountain.
I am going to convert the men of Ca-
thay."

The Old Man of the Mountain laughed
and stroked his beard.

"You had a sermon from Gregory be-
before you came away.   Did he tell you
you were to convert the men of Cathay?"

"He did not."

"Ah, Gregory's a sound man. He knew you can't make saints in a day. Why, child, I've seen the beginning of the world, and I've seen the end of it. I've seen the beginning in a crystal glass, and I've seen the end in a pool of ink in a slave's hand. I've seen mankind begin lower nor the gibbering ape, and I've seen them end the shining sons of God. Millions on millions on millions of years, multiplied unto dizziness, crawling, infinitesimal work overcoming nature, overcoming themselves, overcoming the princes of the powers of darkness, one of whom I am. But this is too deep for you, Marco Polo.

"Now you can go on your way without hindrance from me, Marco Polo, because of the memory of an old time, when the courting of a woman was more to me than the killing of a man, when beauty meant more nor power.

"Let you be on your way, Marco Polo, while I sit here a lonely old man, with wee

soft ghosts whispering to him.  Let you
be hastening on your way before I remember I am a prince of the powers of darkness and should do you harm . . ."

# IX

AND so they went on eastward, ever eastward, and the moons were born, grew, waned, and died . . .

They passed through Khotan, where the divers bring up jade from the rivers, white jade and black jade, and green jade veined with gold. They passed through Camal, the shameful city, whose women are fair and wanton, whose men are cuckolds. And they passed through the province of Chitingolos, where are the mountains of the Salamanders. They passed through the city of Campicha, where there are more idols than men. And they passed through the great city of Samarkand, where the Green Stone is on which Timur's throne was set . . . And moons were born and died . . .

They passed through Tangut, where

the men will not carry the dead out through the door of a house, but must break a hole in the wall. And they passed through Kialehta, where there are snow-white camels. And they passed through the lands of Prester John.

And now they were in the Tatar lands. There passed them lowing musk oxen. There passed them the wild asses of Mongolia. There passed them the barbarians, with their great tents on wheels. There passed them the black-jowled, savage idolaters. There passed them the pretty white-faced women. There passed them huge, abominable dogs.

And they came to the town of Lob, and a new moon arose, and they entered the Desert of the Singing Sands.

## X

WHEREVER they went now was sand, and a dull haze that made the sun look like a copper coin. And a great silence fell on the caravan, and nothing was heard but the crunch of the camels' pads and the tinkle of the camels' bells. And no green thing was seen.

And a great terror fell on the caravan, so that one night a third of the caravan deserted. The rest went on in silence under the dull sun. And now they came across a village of white skeletons grinning in the silent sand. And at night there was nothing heard, not even the barking of a dog. And others of the caravan deserted, and others were lost.

And now they had come so far into the desert that they could not return, but must keep on their way, and on the fifth day

they came to the Hill of the Drum. And
all through the night they could not sleep
for the booming of the Drum. And some
of the caravan went mad there, and fled
screaming into the waste.

And now there was only a great haze
about them, and they looked at one another with terror, saying: "Were we ever
any place where green was, where birds
sang, or there was sweet water? Or maybe we are dead. Or maybe this was all
our life, and the pleasant towns, and the
lamplight in the villages, and the apricots
in the garden, and our wives and children,
maybe they were all a dream that we woke
in the middle of. Let us lie down and
sleep that we may dream again."

But Marco Polo would not let them lie
down, for to lie down was death. But he
drove them onward. And again they
complained: "Surely God never saw this
place that He left it so terrible. Surely
He was never here. He was never here."

And now that their minds were pitched to the heighth of madness, the warlocks of the desert took shape and jeered at them, and the white-sheeted ghosts flitted alongside of them, and the goblins of the Gobi harried them from behind. And the sun was like dull copper through the haze, and the moon like a guttering candle, and stars there were none.

And when the moon was at its full, they came to the Hill of the Bell. And through the night the Bell went *gongh, gongh, gongh,* until they could feel it in every fiber of their bodies, and their skin itched with it. They would stop their ears. But they would hear it in the palms of their hands and the soles of their feet. *Gongh, gongh, gongh.*

And when they left the Hill of the Bell there were only six of the caravan left, and a multitude of white-sheeted ghosts. And the caravan plodded onward dully. And now the warlocks of the desert

played another cruelty. Afar off they
would put a seeming of a lake, and the
travelers would press on gladly, crying,
"There is water! water! God lives! God
lives!" But there was only sand. And
now it would be a green vision, and they
would cry: "We have come to the edge of
the desert. After the long night, dawn.
God lives! God lives!" But there would
be only sand, sand. And now it would be
a city of shining domes in the distance.
And they would nudge one another and
croak, "There are men there, brother, se-
cure streets, and merchants in their
booths; people to talk with, and water for
our poor throats." But there would be
only sand, sand, sand . . . And they
would cry like children. "God is dead!
Have n't you heard? Do n't you know?
God is dead in His heaven, and the warlocks are loosed on the land!"

And on the last day of the moon they
were all but in sight of the desert's edge,

though they did n't know. And the goblins and the warlocks took counsel, for they were now afraid Marco and his few people would escape. They gathered together and they read the runes of the Flowing Sand.

And suddenly the camels rushed screaming into the desert with sudden panic, and a burning wind came, and the sands rose, and the desert heeled like a ship, and the day became night.

And young Marco Polo could stand no more. That was the end, the end of him, the end of the world, the end of everything. There was red darkness everywhere, and he could see nobody. "O my Lord Jesus!" he cried. "O little Golden Bells!" The wind boomed like an organ. The sand screamed. "O my Lord Jesus! O little Golden Bells!" And the voices of his father and uncle were like the tweeting birds. "Where 's the lad, Matthew? Where 's our lad?" "Mark, Mark,

where have you got to? Lad of our
heart, where are you?" But they could n't
find each other. The sand buffeted them
like shuttlecocks. "Boy Mark!" The
sand snarled like a dog; the wind hammered like drums. "Oh, Golden Bells!
O, little Golden Bells! O, my Lord Jesus,
must it end here?"

And the fight went out of him, and a
big sob broke in him, and he lay down
to die . . .

# XI

I SHALL now tell you of Golden Bells, and her in the Chinese Garden.

## XII

I WOULD have you now see her as I see her, standing before Li Po, the great poet, in her green costume. And Li Po, big, fat, with sad eyes and a twisted mouth, uncomfortable as be damned. The sun shone in the garden, the butterflies, the red and black and golden butterflies, flitted from blossom to blossom. And the bees droned. And on the banks of the green lake the kingfisher tunneled his wee house, and the wind shook the blossoms of the apple-trees. And Li Po sat on the marble slab and was very uncomfortable. And in a dark bower was *Sanang*, the magician, brooding like an owl. And Golden Bells stood before Li Po, and there were hurt tears in her eyes.

"Did my father or I ever do anything to you, Li Po, that you should make a

song such as they sing in the market-
place?"

"What song?"

"The Song of the Cockatoo."

"I do n't remember."

"I 'll remind you, Li Po. 'There
alighted on the balcony of the King of
Annam,' the song goes, 'a red cockatoo.
It was colored as a peach-tree-blossom
and it spoke the tongue of men. And the
King of Annam did to it what is always
done to the learned and eloquent. He
took a cage with stout bars, and shut it
up inside.' And was n't that the cruel
thing to write! And are you so impris-
oned here, Li Po? Ah, Li Po, I 'm thinking hard of you, I 'm thinking hard."

"Well, now, Golden Bells, to tell you
the truth th~re was no excuse for it. But
often times I do be feeling sad, and thinking of the friends of my youth who are
gone. Yuan Chen, who might have been
a better poet nor me, if he had been

spared; and H'sieng-yang and Li Chien, too. Ah, they were great poets, Golden Bells. They never sang a poor song, Golden Bells, that they might wear a fine coat. And they 'd write what was true, wee mistress, were all the world to turn from them. And I 'm the laureate now, the court singer, living in my glory, and they 're dead with their dreams. I 'm the last of the seven minstrels. And, wee Golden Bells, I do be thinking long.

"And sometimes an old woman in the street or a man with gray in his hair will lift a song, and before the words come to me, there 's a pain in my heart.

"And I go down to the drinking booths, and the passion of drinking comes on me—a fury against myself and a fury against the world. And the folk do be following me to see will I let drop one gem of verse that they can tell their grandchildren they heard from the lips of Li Po. And when my heart is high with the drinking, I take a lute from a traveling poet, and not knowing what I 'm saying, I compose the song. Out of fallow sorrow bloom the little songs. You must n't be hard on an old man, wee Golden Bells, and he thinking long for his dead friends."

"Ah, poor Li Po," she said, and she had grown all soft again. "Is it so terrible to be old?"

"Now you ask me a question, Golden Bells, and I 'll give you an answer. Besides, it 's part of my duties to teach you wisdom. Now, it is not a terrible thing, at all, at all, to be old. I see the young folk start out in life, and before them there 's the showers of April, there 's wind and heat and thunder and lightning. But I'm in warm, brown October, and all of it 's gone by me. And in a little while I 'll sleep, and 't is I need it, God help me! The old do n't sleep much, wee Golden Bells, so 't is a comfort to look forward to one's rest after the hardness of the world. In a hundred or more years or five hundred, just as the fancy takes me, I'll wake up for a while and wander down the world to hear the people sing my songs, and then I 'll go back to my sleep."

And she was going to ask him another question when the *Sanang* came up. The magician was a thick man with merry eyes and a cruel mouth.

"Golden Bells," he says, "there 's rare entertainment in the crystal glass."

"What is it, *Sanang?*"

"The warlocks of the Gobi have a young lad down, and they 're waiting until the soul comes out of his body. Come, I 'll show you."

And in the crystal glass he showed her Marco Polo, and the knees going from under him in the roaring sands. She gave a quick cry of pity.

"Oh, the poor lad!"

*Sanang* chuckled. "He started out with

a big caravan to preach what he thought was a truth to China. I 've been watching him all along, and it 's been rare sport. I knew it would come to this."

"Could n't you save him, *Sanang?*" she cried. "O, *Sanang,* he 's so young, and he set out to come to us. Could n't you save him?"

"Well, I might." *Sanang* was not pleased. "It 'll be a while before the shadow comes out of him. But it would be rare sport to watch and see the warlocks and the ghouls and the goblins set on it the way terriers do be setting on an otter."

"Oh, save him, *Sanang!* Save him!"

"Now, Golden Bells, I might be able to save him, and again I might n't."

"Save him, *Sanang!*" Li Po broke in. "Save him the way the wee one wants. For if you do n't, *Sanang,* I 'll write a song about you that 'll be remembered for generations, and they 'll point out your grand-

children and your grandchildren's grandchildren, and they 'll laugh and sing Li
Po's song:

" 'There was a fat worm who considered
himself a serpent—' "

"Oh, now, Li Po, for God's sake, let
you not be composing poems on me, for
't is you have the bitter tongue. Promise
me now, and I 'll save him. We 'll send
for the keeper of the khan's drums."

And they sent for the keeper, and *Sanang* gave a message to be put on the
Speaking Drums.

"Let you now," he told his helper, "get
me the Distant Ears."

And the helper brought him the Golden
Ears, which were the like of a great bird's
wings, and he put them on his head and
he listened.

"I hear the drums of the battlements,"
he said, ". . . and I hear the Drums of
the Hill of Graves . . ."

And he listened a while, and Golden Bells was white.

"I hear the Drums of the Dim Mountain," . . . and for a while he said nothing.

"Those would be the drums of Yung Chang . . ."

"I hear the Drums of Kai Yu Kwan," he said.

"Yes, *Sanang,* yes." Little Golden Bells was one quiver of fear.

"I hear the Drums of the Convent of the Red Monks," said *Sanang.* "I hear drums calling the Tatar tribes . . . I hear the slap of saddles. I hear the jingle of bits . . . I hear galloping ponies . . ."

"Yes, *Sanang.* Oh, hurry, *Sanang!* hurry!"

He listened a little while longer, and then he took off the Distant Ears.

"Your man 's saved," he said.

Then little Golden Bells laughed and

then she cried. She caught Li Po's hand
and laughed again and again she cried.
*Sanang* shook his head to get out of his
ears the deafening noises of the world.
And Li Po smiled out of his sad eyes.

"I think I'll go and write a marriage-
song, Golden Bells."

"Whom will you write the marriage-
song for, Li Po?"

"I'll write it for you, Golden Bells."

"But I'm not going to be married, Li
Po. There is no one. I love no one, Li
Po. I do not. I do not, indeed."

"Then take your lute and sing me the
'Song of the Willow Branches,' which is
the saddest song in the world."

She shook her head, and blushed. "I
cannot sing that song, Li Po. I don't
feel like singing that song."

"Then I must write you another song,
Little Golden Bells . . ."

# XIII

AND now when Marco Polo was rested and had recovered, they brought him from the Convent of the Red Monks to where the khan was in the city of Chandu. Now, there were two palaces in Chandu; there was the winter palace, which was of marble, and the summer palace, which was of gilt cane. Around these palaces there was built a wall sixteen miles in compass, and inside of it was a park of fountains, and rivers and brooks with the speckled trout in them, and meadows with the lark at her ease in the grass, and trees of all varieties where the little birds do be building and none to grudge them a home. And all the wild animals were abundant, the timid hare and the wild deer and the wee croaking frogs, long-legged colts by their white mothers, and little dogs tumbling over themselves with the sport of spring. Brown bees among the clover, strawberries in profusion, trees would delight your eyes, and brown cows and black cows, and dappled moilies under the great leaves of them, and lambs would be snowy of fleece. All the flowers of the world were there; the paradise of wild things it was, the park of Kubla Khan.

"In Xanadu did Kubla Khan," quoted young Randall,
"A stately pleasure dome decree,
Where Alph, the sacred river, ran
Through caverns measureless to man,
Down to a sunless sea.
So twice five miles of fertile ground
With walls and towers were girdled round:
And there were gardens, bright with sinuous rills,
Where blossomed many an incense-bearing tree;
And here were forests ancient as the hills,
Enfolding sunny spots of greenery."

"Whose poem is that poem, Brian Oge?"

"It is a poem of Coleridge's, Malachi."

"I though it was maybe a poem of Col-

quitto Dall McCracken of Skye, that one
of you lads had put English on. It is a
poem of the head, you ken, and Colquitto,
being a dark man, could only see with the
eye's ghost. But it has n't the warmth,
the life of the work of Blind Colquitto.
Brian Oge, do you mind the poem Angus
More Campbell of Rathlin wrote to Colquitto Dall?"

" 'Is aoibhinn duid, Colquitto Dall,' "
I remembered: "It is happy for thee,
blind Colquitto, who dost not see much
of women. If thou wert to see what we
see, thou wouldst be tormented even as
I am. My sorrow, O God, that I was not
stricken blind before I saw her amber,
twisted hair!"

"That 's it, that 's it, Brian Oge. But
this is not the place to be talking of
poetry. There is no poetry in this story.

"I will now tell you of Marco Polo and
him entering the presence of the great
khan . . ."

## XIV

AND Marco Polo was brought into the presence. And among all assembled there you could hear a pin drop.

At the north end of the great hall sat the Khan himself, and Marco Polo nearly dropped with surprise; for where he expected a great, magnificent figure of a man, with majesty shining from his eyes, he saw only a pleasant, bearded man, not quarter so well dressed as the meanest servant on the room, and a fine, welcoming smile in his face. His throne was elevated so that his feet were on the level of the heads of the kinsmen of the Blood Royal beneath him, and they in silk and ermine and fine brocades and jewels. And beneath these were the barons and dukes and knights. And beneath these were the captains of the fighting men, three thousand and three. And beneath these were the musicians and the sorcerers. And behind Kubla Khan, very big, very erect, stood his three great servants, the Keeper of the Hunting Leopards, the Keeper of the Speaking Drums, and the Keeper of the Khan's Swords.

And beside Kubla Khan, on a little throne, sat Golden Bells . . . And it was the sight of her more than the sight of the great assembly that dumbed the words in his mouth. And Kubla was smiling at him, and she was smiling, too.

And Kubla saw there was something wrong with him, that there was embarrassment on him, and he rose from his throne.

"There is welcome for you here, Marco Polo, and no enmity. There is interest in and eagerness for your message. There is none here will criticize you or make it hard for you. Let there be no shame on you in speaking before so many people.

Say what you have to say as if there were
nobody here, if that will help you, barring
myself and the little daughter beside
me . . ."

"O Emperor," the words came back to
Marco Polo, "and ye, great princes,
dukes, and marquises, counts, knights, and
burgesses, and people of all degrees who
desire the light of the world, grace be to
you and peace, from God our Father, and
from the Lord Jesus Christ!

"The message I have to give you, I
shall give in the words of Him, Whose
perfect message it is:

" '*Beati pauperes spiritu*,—Blessed are
the poor in spirit.

" '*Quoniam ipsorum est regnum caelo-
rum*,—for theirs is the kingdom of
heaven.

" '*Beati mites*, — Blessed are the
meek. . .' "

And Marco Polo went on and quoted
for them the words that were spoken on

the Mount in Galilee. And they listened to him with great civility and attention. And little Golden Bells leaned forward, with her chin on her hands, and Kubla leaned back in his throne, with his eyes half closed.

" 'But I say unto you, that ye resist not evil, but whoever shall smite thee on the right cheek, turn to him the other also.' " And at this the great Khan looked up puzzled, and a movement went through the fighting men in the hall. But wee Golden Bells never budged a minute, and Marco Polo went on:

" '*Et factum est; cum consummasset Jesus verba haec,*—And it came to pass when Jesus had ended these sayings, the people were astonished at his doctrine.'

"I shall now tell you of the life and death of the Lord Jesus . . ."

He told them of the birth in Bethlehem, and of the teaching on the hills, and the poets nodded their heads; and he told

them of the cleansing of the lepers and
of the casting out of devils and the rais-
ing of Lazarus from the dead, and the
magicians wondered; and he told them of
the betrayal by Judas with a kiss, and the
captains-at-arms shuffled in their seats;
and he told them of the scourging, and of
the crowning with thorns, and the great
Khan snicked his dagger in and out of the
sheath.   And a mist of tears came into the
eyes of Golden Bells.

And he told them of the crucifixion between two thieves, and a great oath ripped
from the beard of Kubla Khan, and the
silver tears ran from the eyes of Golden
Bells.

" 'And on the third day He arose from
the dead . . .' "

And a great shout came from the
throat of Kubla Khan, and he stood up.

"He arose from among the dead men,
I 'll warrant; He showed himself to the

Roman Pilate in all His power and majesty—"

"No," said Marco Palo.

"Then He showed himself to the thousands who had seen him die upon the gallows tree!"

"No," said Marco Polo.

"Who saw Him, then?"

"His twelve Apostles and they in a little room!"

And Kubla Khan sat down suddenly and said no more. There was a moment's murmur of wonder among the assembly, and then silence. And Marco's heart fell. And he was aware of two things, of the great politeness of the Chinese people and of Golden Bell's pitying eyes . . .

# XV

WHEN Kubla Khan dismissed the assembly, and he took Marco Polo into a sitting-room, and Golden Bells came with them.

"And what did you think, sir, of what I said? And can you not see, sir, the truth that 's in me?"

"Well, now, laddie," said the great Khan, "when we come to examine this sermon you quoted to us, what is there in it but the rule of the righteous man? We 've had a great thinker and pious man of our own, Confucius. I 'm not a reading man," says he, "but I 've got an idea," says he, "that there is n't a thing you said but is embraced in the Analects. And if it is n't it 'll be in the teachings of the Lord Buddha."

"Ah, but, sir," Marco Polo said, "you

'll have to admit that He of Whom I speak was the true God made man."

"Now, laddie, remember I'm an old man, set in my head and my ways, and I've been used to one belief so long it would be hard changing. So do n't press me now; do n't press me, I ask you."

"Ah, sir," pleaded Marco Polo, "it's terrible to think of, as great a prince as you to be in the black spaces outside of heaven because you would n't accept the truth."

"Well, maybe they won't be so hard on one, my dear lad. When my time comes and I rap on the gate of your heaven, maybe they'll say: 'It's only old Kubla, the soldier, is in it. He knows devil and all about religion, but his fights were fair fights, and he never hit a man when he was down. He had a soft heart for wee children and he was easy on horses. Sure, what's the difference? Let him in!' And if they say no, I'll tuck the old nicked claymore under my arm, and be off to where the other old fighters are."

"I see, sir, that there was little success to my message."

"I would n't say that," said Kubla Khan. "Wait a little until you perform miracles before the people to prove your truth. You 'll know better then."

"Ah, sir," said Marco Polo, "I can perform no miracles. 'T is only a saint can perform miracles, and I could n't lace a saint's shoes. I have no miracles."

"Oh, well, now, my dear boy," said Kubla Khan, "I hate to tell you, but there 's no use going further. Sure you 'd be up against the sorcerers of the world. They 'd ask you for a sign, and you 'd have no sign, and they'd have signs in abundance. I would n't think of letting you go against them. Fair play 's a jewel, and you would n't have a chance. There 's the Red Pope from Tibet and there's the Black Magician from Korea and a hun-

dred minor ones, and the Warlock of the
North, from the Islands of Ice, who gov-
erns the hail and the snow. Child, I
would n't let you get into the same ring
with them. They 'd ruin you."

"But, sir, was n't it a great miracle of
the Lord's, my rescue in the Gobi
Desert?"

"A miracle of the Lord's! A miracle
of Golden Bells here. It was her magician saw you, and she had the message put
on the drums, and the desert patrols went
to seek you. It was herself here, wee
Golden Bells." And Golden Bells' mouth
gave a smile of shame that his thought
should be broken in his mind.

"A long way I 'm after coming," said
Marco Polo, "and when I set out my
heart was high."

"Now, do n't be taking it too hard,"
says the khan, kindly. "Sure, there 's a
power of good you can be doing here.
Maybe you can do something with Li

Po," says he. "I'd like fine for you to try. The man is worrying the life out of me with his drinking. I never know when he goes out whether he'll come back all right or feet foremost on a door. For he's got the bitter tongue when the drink's in him, and China could ill afford to lose him. And there are some of my captains, and the tune they're always piping is 'War! War! War! And let's show up this Alexander who said he conquered the world.' And I'm past the age when you make war for devilment. So let you be helping me out with them, Marco Polo."

But Marco Polo knew this was only meant in kindness, and his heart was broken.

"Ah, wee lady,"—he turned to Golden Bells,—"wee lady, wee lady, why did n't you let me die in the desert? Why did n't I die?"

"And why should you die, Marco

Polo?" Her low, sweet voice rang in the heart of him. "Did n't you come here to give your message? And to make converts? And did n't I hear your message? And am n't I your convert, Marco Polo?"

# XVI

AND now the place of Li Po was usurped, and gone *Sanang* with his magic glass, and in the jasmine garden by the Lake of Cranes Marco Polo sat and instructed Golden Bells . . . .

## XVII

AND he told of the flight into Egypt when savage Herod reigned, and of the Jewish maid and her child sleeping beneath the shadow of the great Sphinx, while the shades of the old Afric gods looked on in reverence, Amenalk and Thoth and the moon-horned Io, Isis, and Osiris. And the painted kings knelt in their pyramids, and out of the sluggish Nile came the strange aquatic population, the torpid crocodiles and monstrous water lizards, and the great hippopotami lumbered to bow before the little Lord of all things . . .

And he told her how Satan had tempted Him on the lonely, black craigs . . .

"But you are not listening, little Golden Bells—"

"Indeed I am listening, Marco Polo

Yes, indeed I am. I love to hear your voice, Marco Polo. You are so earnest, Marco Polo; there is such a light in your eyes. Listen, Marco Polo, Li Po once wrote a poem, 'White Gleam the Gulls,' and it is the poem by which he is best known, and every time I hear it there is an echo in my heart. But, Marco Polo, I never listened to Li Po's song so eagerly as I am listening to your voice."

"But you are not taking it in, little Golden Bells."

"It is very hard to take in. Marco Polo, It happened so long ago. It is hard to think of a tragedy in a strange country, and we in this garden on the second moon of spring. And it was so very long ago. Do you hear the bees, Marco Polo—the bees among the almond-blossoms? And see the blue heron by the lotus flowers? And do you see the little tortoise, Marco Polo, and he sunning himself on a leaf? If I throw a pebble, Marco Polo, he will dive, and he is such a clumsy diver, Marco Polo!"

"But you must listen, Golden Bells, and believe me."

"I do believe, Marco Polo; I honestly do. Do n't you know I believe you? Anything you say, Marco Polo I believe. You would n't be coming all the way over the world to be telling me a lie. Of course I believe."

"And does n't it make you happy, Golden Bells?"

"Once I was unhappy, Marco Polo. I used sit here, and on my lute I used play the 'Song of the Willow Branches,' which is the saddest song in the world. Under the moon I used be lonely, and the droning of the bees meant nothing to me, and now it is a sweet brave song. I cannot play 'Willow Branches' any more, so alien is sadness to me. And the moon smiles. I am very happy, Marco Polo."

"It is the True Religion, little Golden Bells, that makes you happy."

"Is it, Marco Polo? Is it? It must be, I suppose. I do n't know what it is, but I am very happy."

## XVIII

AND he told her of Paul, who had seen a vision and gone preaching through the world, who was persecuted, who was shipwrecked, who was bitten by a viper, and who survived everything that he might preach the Lord Jesus. He was a fierce, ragged man with burning eyes . . . And he told her of Paul's instructions to women . . .

"You do not look at me when you speak, Marco Polo. Only your voice comes to me, not your eyes. Is it because of Paul?"

And Marco Polo felt great trouble on him, because he could not explain. But Golden Bells went on:

"There is little in your faith about women, Marco Polo. Is it a faith only for men, then? Is it against women?

Must the young men not look at the young women?"

"No, Golden Bells; the young men must not look too much on the young women."

"But that is very foolish, Marco Polo. Is it wrong to see the beauty of the almond blossoms, wrong to taste the scented wind? Is it wrong to watch the kingfisher seeking his nest? Is it wrong to watch the moon, the stars? All these are very beautiful, Marco Polo, so beautiful as to make me cry. Is it wrong to watch them?"

"It is not wrong, Golden Bells. The glory of God is in the beauty of his handicraft."

"Li Po is old and wise and a great poet, Marco Polo, and Li Po says there is beauty in a running horse and beauty in a running stream; but there is no beauty like the beauty of a young woman, and she letting down her hair. God made the beauty of women, too, Marco Polo, as well as the beauty of the stars. Won't you please explain to me, Marco Polo? Why should Li Po say one thing and Saint Paul another?"

"But Golden Bells, Saint Paul is inspired of God."

"But Li Po is inspired of God, too, Marco Polo. You mustn't be thinking little of Li Po. He is fat and old and drunken, but when he sings, Marco Polo, it is the song of the wandering stars. But why must not the young men look at the young women, Marco Polo? Why must they not look with their eyes?"

"It will be hard for me to tell you, Golden Bells—"

"Look at me now, Marco Polo. Lift up your eyes and look into my eyes. Is there evil in me, Marco Polo, that your eyes should avoid me as the fox avoids the dog? Or maybe I am not beautiful. Maybe they told me wrong because I was a king's daughter, and they would not have me think little of myself. Maybe I am not beautiful, Marco Polo, maybe I hurt your eyes.—"

"Ah, Golden Bells, the little horned moon is not more beautiful."

"Then why must not the young men look at the young women, Marco Polo? You are here to instruct me. Won't you tell me why?"

"Maybe—maybe—maybe it is for fear of sin, Golden Bells."

"Sin? Sin! Why should there be sin? I know sin, Marco Polo. They have warned me against it since I crept upon the floor. There are two sins. There is meanness, Marco Polo, and there is cruelty; and those are the only sins. I know your heart, Marco Polo; there is no meanness there. You would not have come here were you mean. The mean do not travel afar for other people. And cruelty! Surely you would not be cruel to me, Marco Polo. You would not be cruel to anybody, dear Marco Polo. You would not be cruel to me?"

"Cruel to you, little Golden Bells! How could I be cruel to you?"

"But the sin, Marco Polo?"

"I don't know, Golden Bells. I don't know."

# XIX

AND one dusk the moon rose over the Chinese garden, and Marco Polo finished telling her of what John saw on Patmos and he an old man . . .

"*Veni, Domine Jesu.*

"*'Gratia Domini nostri Jesu Christi cum omnibus vobis. Amen!*'"

"It is very difficult, Marco Polo. I don't quite understand."

"I don't quite understand myself, Golden Bells. But that is all I can tell you. But you will understand more," he said. "My mission is finished now, and I will go back. I will stop at the court of Prester John, and he will send a bishop surely or some great cardinal to baptize you and to teach you the rest."

"You will go back?" A great pain

stabbed her. "I never thought, somehow, of you as going back."

"I have come on a mission, Golden Bells, and I must go back."

"There is a woman, maybe, in Venice —" And she turned her head away from him and from the moon.

"I would not have you thinking that, Golden Bells. There is none in Venice has duty from me. And if the queen of the world were there, and she pledged to me, I could never look at her, and I after knowing you, Golden Bells!"

"Is it money, Marco Polo?" she whispered in the dusk. "It is maybe your uncle and your father are pressing you to return. Let you not worry then, for my father the great Khan will settle with them, too. There is not a horse in all Tartary that your uncle cannot have, nor a woman, either. And your father can have all the jewels of the treasury, and all the swords, too, even the sword with which my father conquered China. My father will give him that if I ask. Only let you not be leaving this moonlit garden."

"Dear Golden Bells, it isn't that; but I came here for converts—"

"Oh, Marco Polo, listen! There is a folk at Kai-fung-fu, and they are an evil folk and a cowardly folk, and my father abhors them. I shall ask my father to send captains of war and fighting men to convert them to your faith, Marco Polo, or lop off their heads. And we can send a few hundreds to the Pope at Rome, and he will never know how they were converted, and he will be satisfied. Only let you not be going away from me in my moonlit garden. You will only be turning to trade, Marco Polo, and marrying a woman. Let you stay here in the moonlit garden!"

"Ah, little Golden Bells, there is no place in the world like your moonlit garden. There is no place I 'd be liefer than in the moonlit garden. But little Golden Bells, I set out in life to preach the Lord Jesus crucified. It was for that I came to China."

"Let you not be fooling yourself, young Marco Polo. Let you not always be ascribing to God the things that are mine. You did not come to preach to China, you came to see me, and your mind stirred up with the story the sea-captain told, of me playing 'Willow Branches' by the Lake of Cranes. O Marco Polo, before you came there were the moon and the sun and the stars, and I was lonely. O Marco Polo," she cried, "you would n't go, you could n't go! What would you be doing in cold Venice, far from the warm moonlit garden."

"Sure, I 'll be lonely, too, little Golden Bells, a white monk in a monastery, praying for you."

"But I don't want to be prayed for,

Marco Polo." She stamped her foot. "I want to be loved. And there you have it out of me, and a great shame to you that you made me say it, me that was desired of many, and would have no man until you came. And surely it is the harsh God you have made out of The Kindly Person you spoke of. And 'tis not He would have my heart broken, and you turning yourself into a crabbed monk. And how do you know your preaching will convert any? 'Tis few you converted here. Ah, I'm sorry, dear Marco Polo; I should n't have said it, but there is despair on me, and I afraid of losing you."

"'T is true, though. I have nothing, nobody to show."

"You have me. Am n't I converted? Am n't I a Christian? Marco Polo, let me tell you something. I said to my father I wanted to marry you, and I asked him if he would give you a province to govern, and he said, 'Sure and welcome.'

And I asked him for Yangchan, the pleasantest city in all China. And he said, 'Sure and welcome, Golden Bells.' And I told him we would be married, and go there and govern his people kindly. And you wouldn't shame me before my own father, and all the people of China. You couldn't do that, Marco Polo. Marco Polo,"—she came toward him, her eyes shining,—"let you stay!"

"Christ protect me! Christ guide me! Christ before me!"

"Marco Polo!"

"Christ behind me!"

"The moon, Marco Polo, and me, Golden Bells, and the nightingale in the apple-tree!"

"Christ on my right hand! Christ on my left! Christ below me!"

Her arms were around his neck, her cheek came close to his.

"Marco Polo! Marco Polo!"

"Christ above me!"

"My Marco Polo!"

"O, God! Golden Bells!"

And he put his arms around her, and his cheek to hers, and all the battle and the disappointment and the fear and the strangeness went out of him. And down by the lake the wee frogs chirruped, and in the apple-tree the nightingale never ceased from singing. And they stayed there shoulder to shoulder and cheek to cheek. And the moon rose higher. And it seemed only a moment they were there, until they heard the voice of Li Po in the garden.

"Are you there, Golden Bells? Are you there at all, at all? For two hours I've been hunting and could n't get sight or sign of you. I have the new song, Golden Bells. For a long time I was dumb, but a little while ago the power came to me, and I have the new song, Golden Bells, the marrying song. . ."

# XX

"THUS far," said Malachi of the Long Glen, "the story of Marco Polo."

"That is a warm story, Malachi of the Glen, a warm and colored story, and great life to it, and Golden Bells is as alive to me as herself there by the fire, and I can see Marco Polo as plain as I can see my cousin Randall, and he playing with the dogs . . ."

"If they were n't real and live and warm, what would a story be, Brian Oge, but a jumble of dead words? A house with nobody in it, the poorest thing in the world."

"But Marco Polo came back to Venice, Malachi, and fought in the sea-wars."

"There 's more to tell, Brian Oge. But sometimes I wonder should n't the best part of the story be kept to yourself. The people are n't as wise as they used to be, brown lad. The end of a story now is a bit of kissing and courting and the kettle boiling to be making tea.

"But the older ones were wiser, Brian Donn. They knew that the rhythm of life is long and swinging, and that time does n't stop short as a clock. Sure, what is a kiss from the finest of women but a pleasant thing, like a long putt sunk, or the first salmon of the year caught like a trout, or the ball through the goal before the whistle blows? And there 's many a well-filled belly over a hungry soul.

"But a story is how destiny is interwoven, the fine and gallant and the tragic points of life. And you must n't look at them with the eyes of the body, but you must feel with the antennæ of your being. Now, if you were to look at the Lord Jesus with physical eyes, what would it be but a kindly, crazy man and He com-

ing to a hard and bitter end? Look at it
simply, and what was the story of Troy
but a dirty row over a woman?

"But often times the stories with the
endings that grocer's daughters do not be
liking are the stories that are worth while.
And the worth while stories do be lasting.
Never clip a story half-ways because the
Widow Robinson does n't like to have her
mind disturbed, and she warming her
breadth at the fire. The Widow Robinson may have a white coin to buy a book
with, and think you 're the grand author
entirely and you pleasing her. But the
Lord God, who gave you the stories, will
know you for a louse.

"I call to your mind the stories of the
great English writer—the plays of the
Prince of Denmark, and the poor blind
king on the cliff, and the Scottish chieftain
and his terrible wife. The Widow Robinson will not like those stories, and she will

be keeping her white coin . . . But those stories will endure forever . . .

"I will now tell you of Marco Polo, and him leaving China . . .

## XXI

YOU must see him now as he was seventeen years after he had come to China, and fourteen years after his wife, little Golden Bells, had died, a lean figure of a man, with his hair streaked with gray, a lean, hard face on him and savage eyes, and all the body of him steel and whalebone from riding on the great Khan's business, and riding fast and furious, so that he might sleep and forget; but forgetting never came to him . . . You might think he was a harsh man from his face and eyes, but he was the straight man in administering justice, and he had the soft heart for the poor—the heart of Golden Bells. He was easily moved to anger, but the fine Chinese people never minded him, knowing he was a suffering man. Though never a word of Golden Bells came from his mouth, barring maybe that line of Dante's, the saddest line in the world, and that he used to repeat to himself and no one there:

> . . . "*'la bella persona*
> *Che mi fu tolta . . . che mi fu tolta';* who was
> taken from me; Taken! Taken from me!"

And oftentimes a look would come over his face as if he were listening for a voice to speak—listening, listening, and then a wee harsh laugh would come from him, very heartbreaking to hear, and whatever was in his hand, papers or a riding-whip, he would pitch down and walk away . . .

He had just come in from the borders of the Arctic lands, from giving the khan's orders to the squat, hairy tribes who live by the icy shores, and had come to the garden by the Lake of Cranes, the garden where the Golden Bells of singing and laughter were dumb this armful of years, and he was alone, and the listening look was on his face, when there came Kubla and Li Po and the old magician . . .

Now Kubla was very old, so old he could hardly walk, and very frail, and Li Po was very old, too, and gray in the face, and sadder in the eyes than ever, and the magician's white beard had grown to his knees, but there was no more humor in his eyes . . . And Marco Polo helped the old khan to sit down.

"Oh, sir, why did you come to me? Sure I was going to you the moment I had changed my riding-clothes . . . Sir, you should have stayed in your bed . . ."

"There was something on my mind, Marco, and the old do be thinking long to get things off their mind."

"What can I do sir?"

"Marco, my child, you must n't take what I say amiss. But I want you to be going back, to be going back to Venice."

"Sir, what have I done to dissatisfy you? In all my embassies have I been weak to the strong or bullying toward the

weak? Does an oppressed man complain
of injustice, does a merchant complain of
being cheated, or a woman say she was
wronged?"

"Now, Marco of my heart, did n't I
say not to be taking it amiss? Is there
any one closer to me nor you, or is it
likely I 'd be listening to stories brought
against you? It 's just this. I 'm an old
and tired man, Marco Beag, and in a
week or a moon at most I 'm due to die,
so the *Sanang* tells me. Do n't be sorry,
son. Be glad for me. Life has been a
wee bit too long.

"And now, son dear, I want to tell you.
You 've been closer to me than my own
sons, and you 've been the dear lad. And
there 's not one man in all China can say
you did a harsh or an unjust thing; but,
my dear son, 't is just the way of people;
there 's a power of hard feeling against
you in this land, you being a stranger and
having stood so high.

"So when I'm dead, dear son, there's many would do you an injury, and treat you badly; aye, in our family itself, though they smile on you now. Let you be going now, Marco. I'll miss you to close my eyes for me, but my heart will be lighter. It will so. I couldn't sleep easy, and you ill treated in this land of mine. You ask him, too, Li Po."

"Ah, sir," Marco laughed,—"and, Li Po, what is ill treatment to me? Sorrow's my blood brother. What I've suffered! Do you think I could suffer more?"

"I know, Marco, I know."

"Don't you think I suffer now, sir? Fourteen years she's dead now, the wee one who lay by my side in sleep. And never a word and never a sign. In the house where we were married I can see the pool and the willows and the hibiscus, but there is never a token of her," he broke out. "The leaves of trees cover the pavilion, the hair of the musicians is silver, and dust is on the blue and white tiles. And she never comes to comfort me. I can't sleep with waiting. The stars never seem to wane, and the hoar frost comes on the grass, and I'm always waiting. Christ! why should I go back? I've forgotten Venice. I've even forgotten my God for her!"

"*Sanang*," says Kubla Khan to the magician, "couldn't you do something for this poor lad?"

It was now dusk in the garden by the Lake of Cranes . . .

"I don't need any damned wizard to bring my wife to me," raged Marco Polo. "If she were to come, she would come, and I in the dark of the moon and the moorfowl calling. She would have come because my heart needed her." And he raged through the dusk by the Lake of Cranes . . .

"Now, Marco, dear lad, don't be flying off again, but remember that there is science needed to all things. And think, too, that maybe she was not permitted. The older we get, the more we understand the destiny that rules all things, with now a nudge, with now a leading finger, with now a terrible blow over the heart, and what we think at twenty-five was a trifling accident, at seventy-five we know to have been the enormous gesture of God. We are not asked when we like to be born, Marco, nor is it up to us when to die.

"And again, Marco, consider. If she were to have come to you in the dark of the moon-time, in the strange mystic hours when you can hear eternity tick like a clock, your eyes would have been not on this world, but the next. Your look would have been vacant that's now keen to discover injustice. Your body would have been flabby that's now whalebone and steel. And there would have been no memory of you in China, that's now like sweet honey in the mouth.

"Would a wee dead spirit be proud of a man, Marco, and he just crying, crying, crying, and letting the days go by while even the brown bee works, and even the grass grows that cattle may fatten and men eat? She might be sorry, but would there be pride on her? Even a dead woman wants a strong man.

"Now, I'm not saying that the silent dead should not have a voice in our affairs when we need them. But they have wisdom, else what is the use of having died? And if the *Sanang* can bring her, she'll come now and join with us in asking you, now being the time she's needed.

"Child, be guided by us three ancient men. I have lived long and have knowledge of the world. Li Po has lived long and has knowledge of the heart. The *Sanang* has lived long, and knows the secrets of the dead. If to our three voices, who love you, there is added a sign from Golden Bells, will you leave China?"

"If there is a sign from her I 'll leave China," said Marco Polo.

And it was dusk in the Garden by the Lake of Cranes.

# XXII

THE Sanang came over to Marco Polo.

"Give me the black tress that's over your heart."

And Marco Polo undid his coat and his undercoat and his fine sark and took out the perfumed hair, and gave it to the *Sanang*.

"Let you sing a little song, Li Po," the magician said, "the way she'll be hearing and come. I have part of her here, and let you put in the garden the atmosphere she loved." And Li Po took his lute and plucked gently at the strings.

"The swish of your silken skirt is discontinued,"

he sang,

"And the grass grows through the broken hearth
        stone,
And your room that was so warm and swept is
        cold and mouldy.
But he, the beloved of your heart, clings on,

A fallen leaf in the chink of a door,
In the chink of a closed door!"

And it was dusk in the garden, and the
voice of Li Po broke, and his lute stilled,
and the old Emperor breathed his aged
gentle breathing, and the *Sanang* said his
secret terrible formulæ, and Marco Polo
was tense as a hunting dog.

And suddenly at the end of the garden,
in the perfumed Asian dusk, there was a
beam like moonlight, and into the soft
ray of it trod little Golden Bells, with
her wee warm face, and her wee warm
hands, and her hair dark as a cloud, and
her eyes pleading, pleading . . .

"Go now, Marco Polo, please go!"
Her lips made the words, but no sound
came to him.

"Oh, Golden Bells, Golden Bells!" he
rushed forward, but the moonlight of no
moon faded, and there was nothing, and
he dropped on his knees sobbing in the
dusk by the Lake of Cranes . . .

# XXIII

AND after a while he got up from
his knees and set his teeth on his
sobbing and threw his head back and
squared his shoulders and notched his belt
and faced the three ancient men.

"Well," he said, "that's that."

He went over and knelt and kissed the
Khan's hand.

"You'll be seeing her soon, sir, you'll
be telling her . . . everything . . ."

"Yes, son, I'll tell her."

Then he patted the *Sanang* on the shoulder, and "Thanks!" said he, simply, and
he took Li Po's hand in both his, and
they looked at each other for a moment
and no words came to either.

"Well," he says at length, "I'll be hitting the road then. I'll not say good-by
to any of you. I'll be seeing you all pret-

ty soon again. There's a war on between
Venice and the Genoese, and where that's
hottest you'll find me, and the quicker my
end, the better I'll be pleased. But it
would be like my luck," he said bitterly,
"not to be killed, but to be taken prisoner
and to end my life in some lousy jail. Oh,
well, we'll hope for the best." He
laughed. "So—so long!"

And the four of them looked at one another, trying to smile, and great grief on
them.

"China will miss you, my son," said old
Kubla.

"It's nothing to how I'll be missing
China," said Marco Polo. "Venice! It's
only a sound to me. I'll be an exile in
the city of my birth. But what's the use
of complaining? If it's go, it's go. But
it'll be funny," said he. "My body will
be there, but my heart and mind will be
in China. There'll be a gray eye always
turning to China, and it will never see

China . . . Queer! . . .All the voices
and all the instruments in Saint Mark's,
and in my ears the little drums of China
. . . All the sunlight will be glinting on
the Grand Canal, but the little rain of
China—the little rain of China will be
falling in my heart . . .

"Ah, well, if it 's go, it 's go. I 'd better be hitting the road. So . . . I 'll say
good-by for the present . . . and . . .

"Oh, my God Almighty! . . ."

(33)

## THE END

### OF

### MESSER MARCO POLO